GEORGE
AND THE
DRAGON WORD

GEORGE
AND THE
DRAGON WORD

DIANNE SNYDER

ILLUSTRATED BY BRIAN LIES

Houghton Mifflin Company
Boston   1991

Library of Congress Cataloging-in-Publication Data

Snyder, Dianne.
    George and the dragon word / Dianne Snyder ; illustrated by Brian Lies.
        p. cm.
    Summary: When George turns Greataunt Agatha into a dragon by shouting an ugly magic word, the twosome visits Wordsworth to exchange the word for one which will reverse the spell.
    ISBN 0-395-55129-3
    [1. Vocabulary—Fiction. 2. Behavior—Fiction. 3. Magic—Fiction. 4. Greataunts—Fiction.] I. Lies, Brian, ill.
    II. Title.
PZ7.S685175Ge 1991   90-23394
[Fic]—dc20   CIP
                             AC

Text copyright © 1991 by Dianne Snyder
Illustrations copyright © 1991 by Brian Lies

Printed in the United States of America

BP 10 9 8 7 6 5 4 3 2 1

For Ryan and Kristina
and Ellen MacMurray — Ishkabibble!
— D.S.

GEORGE
AND THE
DRAGON WORD

Chapter One

George had a certain word he used when he got mad. It was short and sharp and ugly. It sounded like hissing and spitting at the same time. It had an almost magical power to make people cry.

One day George's parents took a vacation and Greataunt Agatha came to stay. She brought two red suitcases and a hatbox. She brought knitting needles, three bags of wool, and a green parakeet in a yellow cage.

She also brought a picture book with a red dragon on the cover. The dragon had green eyes like Greataunt Agatha's. The book was for George and his sister, Beth. But everything else was Greataunt Agatha's.

1

Greataunt Agatha took her suitcases to George's parents' room. She pushed their clothes to one side of the closet and filled the space with her own. She put her brush and comb and hairpins on his mother's dressing table. She put her hatbox on his father's bureau. And she put her parakeet on the living room coffee table, right where George played with his space cadets.

George poked his finger into the cage and pushed the swing where the bird sat. The parakeet squawked and flapped his wings.

"He doesn't like to be jiggled," said Greataunt Agatha.

"I'm not jiggling," said George. "I'm helping him swing."

"He doesn't like it," Greataunt Agatha said louder.

The parakeet pecked at George's finger.

"Ouch!" cried George.

"You see?" said Greataunt Agatha. "Pretty bird," she cooed at the parakeet.

George thought of the ugly magic word. But he didn't say it.

Next morning, Greataunt Agatha made poached eggs on toast for George and Beth.

George stared at the poached egg.

"George only eats scrambled eggs," said Beth.

"I'm sure George will like poached egg, too, if he gives it a chance," Greataunt Agatha said.

To give the egg a chance, Greataunt Agatha cleared away all the breakfast plates except George's. George

stabbed the egg with his fork. The yolk oozed over the side of the plate.

"He's not going to eat it, Aunt Agatha," said Beth.

"If he wants to go play, he'll eat it," Greataunt Agatha said firmly.

George glared. The ugly magic word drummed in his head. But he didn't say it. Forty minutes later, he ate the egg. It tasted every bit as bad as he expected.

Greataunt Agatha made rules. They were for George and Beth, she said. But George was sure they were mostly for him. All the rules began with *Don't*.

1. Don't poke at the parakeet.
2. Don't jump on the bed.
3. Don't kick under the table.

"Don't play in the hall, George. You get in the way," Greataunt Agatha said. She was on her way to the washroom with a load of laundry.

"Always *don't*," George muttered, and the ugly magic word drummed in his head again. He stomped off to Beth's room.

Beth was sitting on the bed with her friend Sue Ann. They were reading the new picture book with the

dragon on the cover that Greataunt Agatha had brought.

"Let me see." George grabbed at the book.

"Don't!" Beth and Sue Ann pulled it away.

"It's my book too," George cried.

"We had it first," said Beth. "Besides, it's too hard for you." Beth was two years older than George. She considered every book she read too hard for him.

"It is not. Let me see!"

"Wait your turn." Beth held the book up close so that only she and Sue Ann could see the page.

"Give it to me!" George lunged for the book and gave a yank. It fell to the floor with an awful rip.

The next moment Greataunt Agatha walked in. Two red spots shone on her cheeks like warning lights at the scene of an accident.

"Who did that?"

She pointed to the book. The cover was half torn off, and a jagged crack cut between the dragon's green eyes.

"George grabbed it," said Beth.

"George tore it," said Sue Ann.

"It was my turn to read and you wouldn't let me," George shouted. The ugly magic word pounded in his head.

"I would too, but you always grab," wailed Beth. She turned to Greataunt Agatha. "George ruins everything."

George opened his mouth and spat out the ugly magic word. Beth shrieked and burst into sobs. He spat it again. Sue Ann wailed. Both girls ran from the room.

"Obstreperous boy! Look what you've done!" Greataunt Agatha shook her finger at George.

George spat the ugly magic word at her too. Her jaw began to tremble.

Good! George thought. She's going to cry.

But Greataunt Agatha did not cry. Instead her cheeks turned flaming red. The color spread over her face like fire. Her breath sizzled. Even her green eyes seemed to be burning. Now she began to swell. Bigger and bigger and bigger.

George gasped. She was turning into something that was not Greataunt Agatha at all. He closed his eyes tight and yelled the ugly magic word as loud as he could. Surely, that would take care of her. He opened his eyes.

Greataunt Agatha had turned into a dragon, just like the dragon in the book.

In a flash the dragon's claws locked around George's wrist.

"Let me go!" George pulled with all his might, but the claws only grew tighter.

"Let me go!" He kicked at the dragon's feet. The dragon lashed back with its tail. He yelled the ugly magic word again.

The dragon roared with fury, "I'll fix you!"

Before George knew what was happening, the dragon had dragged him out the front door, down the elevator, and into the street.

Chapter Two

People scattered like bowling pins as George and the dragon sped by.

"Help!" cried George.

But no one tried to stop the dragon. The iron grip on George's wrist held him fast. He galloped to keep up. The dragon's tail slapped his heels to spur him on.

He was all out of breath when they stopped at last. In front of them was a heavy door with a gold knocker. The dragon pulled the knocker once, very loudly, and stormed in without waiting for an answer.

"Wordsworth!" the dragon roared. "Wordsworth, where are you?"

The room they entered was full of books. Books on

the chairs, the floor, everywhere. There were letters of the alphabet, too. In the corner was a desk littered with crumpled paper and pencil shavings.

Nobody seemed to be home except a gray tabby cat curled on some books at the window. The cat opened a sleepy eye and looked at George. Then it saw the dragon.

"Eeeow!" The cat sprang up in such a fright it knocked two books to the floor. It scrambled for cover under the desk.

"Thunderation!" cried a voice. "What the devil's going on out there?"

A man hurried in from a back room. He looked like a wise old ram. He had a long face and white hair that curled like a ram's horn on both sides of his forehead. A pair of spectacles perched at the end of his long nose. He pushed them up when he saw the dragon.

"Wordsworth, it's me, Agatha," the dragon cried. The man stared.

"It's me," the dragon cried again. "Help me, Wordsworth! Help me! You see what a state I'm in."

Wordsworth pushed his spectacles as close to his

13

eyes as they would go and peered at the dragon.

"Agatha?" He shook his head. He moved the spectacles to the tip of his nose and peered again. "I don't believe it."

"It's all because of this boy."

The claw on George's arm unlocked at last. The dragon shoved him forward for Wordsworth to see.

Wordsworth adjusted his spectacles again and peered at George. "Who are you?"

The dragon answered before George could open his mouth. "He's George, my niece's boy. She and her husband are away on vacation and I'm taking care of the children."

"How very kind of you," said Wordsworth. "I'm sure it isn't easy."

"You have no idea!" The dragon's eyes flashed indignantly. "I do my best to keep order. Believe me, there's plenty to do. And Beth has been a help. But George . . ." The dragon's voice rose sharply. "George has been simply awful."

George felt his head begin to pound as if an angry fist were inside.

"Simply awful," the dragon repeated. "He teases, he breaks things, he won't obey. And worst of all, he says the most horrid word."

Wordsworth looked at George. The pounding in George's head grew louder.

"A filthy word!"

"It's not. It's magic!" George shouted.

"A disgusting word!"

"It's my word, and I'll say it whenever I want," George cried. And he said the ugly magic word again. And again. And again.

The dragon gave a fearful shriek. It would have pounced on George that instant if Wordsworth had not blocked the way.

"Let me by!" The dragon lashed its tail at the desk. Paper and pencils scattered across the floor. The tabby cat ran out from under the desk yowling.

"Make him stop!" The dragon's tail lashed again. A display of alphabet letters crashed to the floor.

"Here, here! We can't have this," Wordsworth cried.

"Make him stop!"

"I will, I will," he said hurriedly.

"This instant!" The tail whipped at the air inches from George. His knees shook as he ducked behind Wordsworth.

"I'll do my very best," Wordsworth said, "but you must give me time."

Then, to George's surprise, he put his arm around the dragon and began to pat its back.

"You know, my dear," he said in a soothing voice, "the hat shop at the corner is having a sale just now. Spring hats, I believe." As he spoke, Wordsworth

16

steered the dragon gently but firmly to the door.

"They've got a lovely yellow one in the window."

"Yellow?" The dragon's tail paused in midair.

"Canary yellow." He smiled. "I've always thought that color especially nice on you." He opened the door.

The dragon looked at the door, then at Wordsworth, then at George.

"That ugly word had better be gone when I get back."

"It will," said Wordsworth.

"It won't," said George. But he spoke very softly.

Chapter Three

The room was suddenly quiet now that the dragon had gone. George's knees stopped shaking.

Wordsworth began picking up the papers and pencils the dragon had knocked to the floor. George helped. The papers, he noticed, had only a few words written on them, and most of those were crossed out. He didn't recognize any of the words.

George put the papers and pencils back on the desk and waited to see what Wordsworth would do next. He didn't look as though he meant any harm. Still, his mildness could be a trick.

Wordsworth frowned. He took off his spectacles and cleaned the lenses with his handkerchief. Then he held them up to the light, put them back on, and cleared his throat. He did not look at George.

"Samuel," he called. "Samuel, I need you."

The tabby cat crept out warily from behind a stack of books. When he saw George, he stopped short and hissed.

"There, there, Samuel!" Wordsworth hurried over and lifted Samuel in his arms. "There's nothing to be afraid of now."

Wordsworth motioned George to come nearer. Samuel glared at him to stay away.

"Samuel was named after Samuel Johnson, who wrote the first English dictionary."

"I was named after Saint George," said George.

"Ah, yes, the fellow who killed the dragon," said Wordsworth. "A good namesake, don't you agree, Samuel?"

Samuel squirmed to be let down. Wordsworth released him with a sigh.

"I'm afraid Samuel is not very sociable," he said. "It's my fault. I spend so much time just sitting and thinking. Samuel has picked up my habits."

George looked at Samuel. He was back at his old perch, staring out the window.

"Does Samuel think too?" George asked.

"Oh, my, yes! He's a deep thinker."

"What is he thinking?"

Wordsworth lowered his spectacles to study the question.

"I believe he's thinking about that word you used."

To George's surprise, Wordsworth said the ugly magic word. The word that made Beth and Sue Ann cry and Greataunt Agatha turn into a dragon.

"Initial fuster, did you notice, Samuel?" said Wordsworth.

"Nishul what?" George asked.

"Fuster," the man repeated. "Your word begins with a fuster."

George frowned.

"It's simple. Fusters are sounds you make by blowing air. *Shhh . . . thhh . . . fff —*"

"*Ssss!*" The cat hissed.

Wordsworth looked very pleased. "Right you are, Samuel. *Ssss* is a fuster too.

"They're all the rage these days," he continued. "They're so handy for letting off steam. Everyone wants one. I couldn't stay in business without them."

"Business? What business?" George felt very confused.

"The business of making words. I'm a wordsmith, you know."

"What words?"

"Any words." The wordsmith laughed. "I'll make a word for:

> an enemy,
>
> a recipe,
>
> a lover's plea,
>
> a strain of flu,
>
> a stringy stew,
>
> a dance that's new,

. . . whatever the customer wants."

He waved his arm at the shelves along the walls. "Those are all words I made."

George looked at the shelves. Now he noticed a curious thing. They were filled with letters of the alphabet in all sizes. The letters stood in groups, like model trains on display. Each group had its own style. One had round orange letters. Another, thin slanted ones. Were these words?

"I thought words go in dictionaries," George said. "Beth has a dictionary and it's got words."

"They do go in dictionaries," Wordsworth agreed. "But first they have to be invented. And then they have to be used. The dictionary makers are strict about that. They won't accept a word that isn't used."

He bent down and picked up some shiny white letters that the dragon had knocked to the floor.

"What word is that?" asked George.

"Globble." Wordsworth dusted the letters on his sleeve before setting them back on the shelf. "It's one of my newest creations. It means talking with your mouth full. Mothers find it very useful," he added.

"Mine doesn't," said George.

"Maybe you could tell her," the wordsmith said hopefully. "*Don't globble* is much easier to say than *Don't talk with your mouth full*."

"I'd rather not," said George.

Wordsworth looked disappointed. "Perhaps you'd like this one." He pointed to a row of tall orange letters. "Ishkabibble. I find it very handy."

"What does it mean?"

"It doesn't mean anything," said Wordsworth. "That's the beauty of it."

24

"Then what's it for?"

"For nonsense things or things people say that you don't believe. For instance, what if someone tells you he's a Martian?"

"I'd tell him he's crazy," said George.

25

"Ishkabibble!" said the wordsmith. "The thing to say is *ishkabibble*." He leaned close to George and whispered in his ear, "There's a bag of pirate's gold buried under this floor. What do you say to that?"

"Ishkabibble!" said George.

"There, you have it." He looked very pleased.

"Here's another I think you'll like." He pointed to a set of purple letters that tilted slightly backward.

"Scrutch," George read. "What's it for?"

"Mistakes. The next time you miss a ball or you hammer your finger instead of a nail, say *scrutch*. It will make you feel better."

"Will it work for Beth, too?"

"It works for anyone."

George pointed to the next shelf up. It held a black box with a padlock on it.

"What's in that?"

"A special word I made to order for a clown."

"Why is it locked up?"

"Because it's not for just anyone," said Wordsworth. "Certain words are like that, you know. They have special powers."

George thought of his ugly magic word. "Like making people cry?" he asked.

"Like that," said the wordsmith.

"Or turning someone into a dragon?" said George.

"That can happen too. Words don't always work the way you expect."

Suddenly, George had an idea. "Can you make a word that gets rid of dragons?"

Wordsworth peered at George over the top of his spectacles. "Do you have a particular dragon in mind?"

"Oh, no particular one." George tried to sound as if the question hardly mattered. "As long as it works for she-dragons."

"I see."

Wordsworth sat down at his desk and moved his spectacles lower on his nose. It occurred to George that he pulled them down when he was thinking and pushed them up when he was looking at something. Right now, they sat near the tip of his long nose. He must be thinking hard, George decided.

After a time the wordsmith pushed his spectacles

midway up and cleared his throat. "Let me see if I have this right. You want me to make a word that will get rid of the dragon."

"Right," said George.

"Your Greataunt Agatha wants me to get rid of the word that turned her into a dragon."

"Right," said George.

"So you both want the same thing — no more dragons."

"Right," said George. "No more dragons."

"Good! Very good!" Wordsworth leaned back and gave a big smile. "By George! George, I believe you and I can do business."

Chapter Four

Wordsworth pulled up a chair for George to sit beside him. Then he took out a pad of lined yellow paper and a nubbly pencil and cleared a place on his desk.

"Now, how shall we do this? A dragon word is not easy to make, you understand. There are many things to consider. Do you want a short word or a long one?"

"Short," George said. "But not too short."

"A prickly word or a smooth one?"

"Prickly."

Wordsworth frowned ever so slightly. "A light word or a heavy one?"

"Heavy," said George.

Wordsworth paused. "If a dragon is attacking, you

need to act quickly. A heavy, prickly word can be slow on the tongue. Of course, it's your word and if you prefer —"

"What if it's light and prickly?"

"That would be better," said Wordsworth. He scrawled some words on the pad.

"Now, let's consider rhythm. Do you want a word

that goes *ta-TA* or one that goes *TA-ta?*"

"Which one works best for dragons?" George asked.

"I suggest *ta-TA*. It's more dramatic." He added another note to his pad.

"Now, the special effects. That's a complicated business. I have to fix your word so that it works only for you. And only on dragons."

"She-dragons," George corrected him.

"She-dragons," said Wordsworth. "How soon do you need this word?"

"Right away," George said.

"Hmmm. Urgent, special order with executionary powers," Wordsworth muttered as he wrote. He lowered his spectacles when he was done and peered at George over them.

"That's a top-quality word you're asking for. Not cheap, I'm afraid."

"I have fifty cents in my pocket," George said.

Wordsworth frowned. "A top-quality word is worth at least a dollar."

George turned his pockets inside out to see if any

more money was tucked away. But fifty cents was all he found.

The wordsmith took off his spectacles and tapped them against the palm of his hand.

"Suppose we arranged a trade," he said.

"What sort of trade?"

"I give you a word that gets rid of dragons and you give me a word in return."

"What word?"

"You know." Wordsworth said the ugly magic word, the word that had made Beth and Sue Ann cry and Greataunt Agatha turn into a dragon.

"Give it up and you can have the new word in exchange."

"Give it up for good?"

Wordsworth nodded.

"But it's *my* word. And it's magic."

"Magic or not, think what trouble it has caused," said Wordsworth.

"What trouble? It works perfectly."

"Does it? Look what it did to your Aunt Agatha."

"She made me mad," said George. "Besides, it doesn't usually work that way. It never did before."

"You won't have accidents like that with my word," said the wordsmith. "If I make a word that gets rid of dragons, I guarantee it will work."

George sighed heavily. How could he give up his ugly magic word? It was so sharp, so strong. And it made him feel so powerful. Still, it would be nice to have a word that didn't make everyone mad at him. And, oh, it would certainly be nice to be rid of the dragon.

"Well?" Wordsworth had put his spectacles back on and was tapping his pencil. George saw that he had written a large *o* in the center of a clean sheet of paper.

"Can you make my new word strong?"

"As strong as an elephant." He wrote an *a*.

"Can it have *shhh, thhh, fff, sss?*"

"Fusters?" said Wordsworth. "Yes, I'll give it a good strong fuster." He wrote an *f*.

"Two," said George.

"You drive a hard bargain." He added an *s*. "Now, is it a trade?"

"Hmmm," said George. "It's a little short."

"I could add a smacker or two," said Wordsworth.

"What's that?"

"A sound you make by smacking your lips."

"What kind have you got?"

"Oh, there's *b* and *p* and *m* —"

"Add *p* and *m*."

"Done! Is it a trade?"

"Done," said George.

"Excellent!" cried Wordsworth. "Now, one last thing. Do you intend to say this word in a soft voice or a loud one?"

"Loud," said George. "Very loud."

"Then you'll need an exclamation point," Wordsworth said. "It goes at the end. There!" He looked very pleased as he held out the pad for George to see.

"I'll get your letters now. You'll want them in a box for safekeeping, I assume." Wordsworth got up and disappeared into the back room.

George waited. For a minute everything was still. Then a piercing hiss made him jump to his feet. It was Samuel. He was staring out the window, his eyes as big as pinwheels. His back was arched in terror.

Coming up the street, not ten steps away, was the dragon.

Chapter Five

"Help!" George cried.

The dragon gave a knock that shook the whole doorframe. The air crackled like lightning. Samuel leaped from the window and scurried under the desk. George was about to crawl under it himself when he remembered the new dragon word. Just in time, he shouted it as loudly as he could.

The door flew open with a bang. There stood Greataunt Agatha wearing a yellow hat with a red poppy flopped over the brim.

"It works!" cried George.

"Of course it works." Wordsworth had returned to the room. In his hand was a shiny silver box, like a lunch box, with a red handle.

"What works?" Greataunt Agatha blinked her eyes as if she had just awakened from a long nap.

"Why, your new hat, my dear." Wordsworth winked at George. "It suits you even better than I imagined."

Greataunt Agatha looked very pleased. She tilted her head to give a different view. "You don't think the poppy is a little too —"

"It's splendid," said Wordsworth. He handed the silver box to George.

"Splendid," said George.

Greataunt Agatha beamed. Then she noticed the box. "What's in that?"

"A word," said George.

"What word?"

"My new magic word." He opened the lid a crack, just enough so he could see inside but Greataunt Agatha couldn't.

"But I brought you here to get rid of a word," said Greataunt Agatha.

"We did get rid of it," said Wordsworth. He pointed to some shelves at the back of the room. There, in a dark corner of the top shelf, stood George's old ugly magic word. The letters were steely gray, and they pointed inward like a shark's teeth.

"Horrid thing!" Greataunt Agatha shivered. "I'm glad it's gone. But, Wordsworth, why did you give him another?"

"If you take something away from someone, you must give something in return," he said mildly.

"Otherwise, it wouldn't be fair, would it?"

He pushed his spectacles flat up against his face and peered hard at Greataunt Agatha. Her cheeks reddened just a tinge.

"I hope you intend to keep this word to yourself," she said to George.

"Of course," said George. "That's why I've got it locked in a box."

"Are you sure it won't cause trouble?"

"Positive," said George.

"It's fully guaranteed and made to order," said Wordsworth. "George was very particular about that."

"He was?" Greataunt Agatha looked surprised.

"He struck a good bargain, too."

"He did? What did it cost?" She opened her purse. Wordsworth brushed it aside.

"No cost to you, my dear. George has taken care of everything."

Greataunt Agatha's eyes widened. She looked at George. "Well!" she said.

He gave her a small smile.

"Well, well . . ."

"Will that be all, my dear?" said the wordsmith.

Greataunt Agatha nodded and reached for George's hand. "I always did think you were a smart boy," she said.

Chapter Six

Beth and Sue Ann were sprawled on the floor when George and Greataunt Agatha got home. They scrambled to their feet. They'd been eating cookies. There were crumbs on the rug.

"Aunt Agatha got a new hat," said George.

"Oooh! It's pretty," said Beth.

"Oooh!" said Sue Ann.

Greataunt Agatha took off the hat so that they both could admire it. George sat down on the sofa and put the silver box beside him.

"What's that?" Beth asked.

"My new magic word."

"Can I see?"

George shook his head. He put the box on his lap

for safekeeping.

"Aunt Agatha, what's in that box?" said Beth.

"A word," said Greataunt Agatha.

"What word?"

"I don't know. But if it's anything like the old word, a box is the best place for it."

"I bet there isn't anything in it," Beth scoffed.

George picked up the box and opened it just a crack. "Yes, there is," he said. And he gave it a little jiggle so Beth could hear things move inside.

"Let me see," cried Beth. Before George could snap shut the lid, she grabbed it by the handle. The bottom fell open, and six red letters and an exclamation point scattered onto the floor.

Beth gave a shout of triumph. "It's fompas," she cried.

"Pomfas," said Sue Ann.

They both looked at George. "Which way does it go?" Beth asked.

George didn't answer. He was busy picking up the letters.

"Smopfa! Is it smopfa? Tell me, George," Beth demanded.

George didn't answer.

"Aunt Agatha, make him tell me!" Beth was shouting now.

Greataunt Agatha shook her head. "It's George's word. If he wants it to be a secret, then it's no business of ours."

But Beth was determined. "It's mafops, isn't it, George?"

George put the last of the letters into the box.

"Tell me, George!"

He shut the lid tight.

"All right. Don't tell me. I'll get it anyway," cried Beth.

"Ishkabibble!" said George.

"Oh, look! What's that?" Beth reached under the sofa and gave a triumphant cry. "I have it!"

"Have what?" George was puzzled. All six letters were back in the box. He had counted them as he picked them up. What could Beth have found?

"I've got the *i*," she announced.

"What *i*?" said George. "There's no *i* in my word."

"Ha! You can't trick me," said Beth. She opened her hand. There was the exclamation point, upside down.

"Now I know all the letters. I'll figure it out for myself."

She handed the exclamation point to George. "It's pifomas, isn't it?" she said. George smiled.

"Pofimas?" said Sue Ann. George's smile grew wider.

"Simpofa?"

"Fopsima?"

"Will you tell us if we guess right?"

"Of course!" George grinned.

He knew they never would.